W9-CHK-897

# A GIANT
# CAN DO ANYTHING

*Other books by Eric Houghton*

THE WHITE WALL
THEY MARCHED WITH SPARTACUS
SUMMER SILVER
BOY BEYOND THE MIST
THE MOUSE AND THE MAGICIAN

# A GIANT
# CAN DO ANYTHING

*Story by* ERIC HOUGHTON

*Pictures by* FAITH JAQUES

ANDRE DEUTSCH

*For the boys and girls of*
*Elphinstone Junior School, Hastings.*

First published 1975 by
André Deutsch Limited
105 Great Russell Street  London WC1

Copyright © 1975 by
Eric Houghton and Faith Jaques
All rights reserved

Printed in Great Britain by
Colour Reproductions Ltd  Billericay  Essex

ISBN 0 233 96237 9

Jeremy lived on a farm. All round it were corn-fields, hills and woods. There was a river too, not far away.

One day Jeremy put on his strongest shoes and his oldest jumper and went out exploring. He ran out of the farmyard, then past the two empty barns – and all at once found himself lying in the grass. He had tripped over the roots of the fat oak-tree. It grew too near the path, and Jeremy's father kept saying he must find time to chop it down one day.

Jeremy picked himself up and rubbed the new bump on his head. Then he ran on through the corn-fields. He crossed the river by a wooden bridge and entered a thick wood. It was called Grumff's Wood. Nobody knew why.

It was an interesting wood. Sometimes the trees grew so tall you couldn't see their tops. Sometimes the bushes grew so close you could hardly squeeze through. And sometimes you found a glade, quite empty of trees and bushes but covered with soft bright grass.

Jeremy was a good explorer. In one glade he found three rabbit-holes. In another glade he found some mushrooms. And in the third glade he found a giant.

The giant was lying asleep on the grass. But when Jeremy stepped on a twig that went *snap*, the giant awoke.

First he opened one eye. Then he opened the other. Each of them was almost as large as Jeremy's head. When he saw Jeremy, the giant blinked and sat up.

"How do you do?" said Jeremy. "I'm called Jeremy."

The giant rubbed his eyes sleepily. "Grumff," he yawned.

"I've never met a giant before," said Jeremy. "What's *your* name?"

The giant scratched his untidy hair. "Grumff," he mumbled.

"I wish I was a giant, Mr Grumff," Jeremy said. "A giant can do lots of things – useful things. If you wanted to start a zoo, you could walk to Africa and catch some elephants in your hands, couldn't you? And if you wanted to be a farmer, you wouldn't need big carts to carry all your corn in at harvest-time. You could take it all at once in one huge armful. Things like that take my Dad ever so long." Jeremy rubbed the new bump on his head. "He's been wanting to chop down that oak-tree near the barns for months – but he can never find enough time. So it tripped me up today and gave me this."

"Grumff," said the giant. He yawned and began to lie down again.

Then he gave a tremendous roar and jumped up. He popped his finger into his mouth and sucked it hard. Big tears came into his eyes and rolled down his cheeks.

Jeremy saw the prickly hawthorn bush where the giant had been lying. "If you take the thorn out quickly, Mr Grumff," he said, "it won't hurt so much."

The giant took his finger from his mouth. There was a sharp thorn stuck in the tip.

"Grumff," groaned the giant.

"Go on, Mr Grumff," said Jeremy. "Take it out."

The giant tried. And he tried again. And again.

And do you know what he discovered? He discovered that his giant's fingers were too big to get hold of that tiny thorn.

Then he tried several times with his teeth. But he discovered that his teeth were too big as well.

"Grumff," he moaned. He took out his handkerchief and dabbed his tears. Sadly he sat down on the grass again.

Jeremy felt so sorry for the giant that he climbed up on to his huge hand and walked along his finger. "You must keep very still, Mr Grumff," he said. He gripped the thorn with his own small fingers and pulled it out.

"Oo," said the giant. And as soon as Jeremy had jumped down to the grass, he popped his finger into his mouth for a quick suck. Then he smiled at Jeremy and nodded happily.

"Grumff-grumff!" he exclaimed.

"Not at all, Mr Grumff," said Jeremy. "Please don't mention it." He put the thorn safely in his pocket.

The giant gave an enormous yawn and stretched his arms sleepily up into the sky.

"I think I'd better go back now," said Jeremy. "I'm sorry I woke you up, Mr Grumff. Perhaps you'll be awake when I come tomorrow. Good-bye."

Jeremy began to walk home. He stopped for a minute on the wooden bridge and looked down into the river. "I'm glad I found a giant," he told it. "Of course, he can't speak our language; but that doesn't matter, because he understands everything I say. Giants are useful, you know. They're so big and strong, they can do anything – anything they like."

Then he felt the sharp thorn in his pocket and said, "Well – almost anything."

He dropped the thorn into the river and went home.

\*    \*    \*

The next morning Jeremy was woken by the sound of a motor. He jumped out of bed and peeped from his window. Down in the farmyard his father was testing the harvester.

Jeremy dressed quickly. He liked watching the harvester. Every year his father drove the tractor round and round the corn-fields and the harvester dragged along behind, cutting the ripe corn. Jeremy sometimes helped to pile the corn-sheaves inside the two barns. He hurried downstairs.

"Good morning, Jeremy," said his father. "Did you hear the rough wind last night?"

Jeremy thought carefully. He couldn't remember hearing anything. "No, Dad," he said. He sat down at the breakfast table.

"When I went out early this morning," said his father, "I found that fat oak-tree lying on its side, well away from the path. I'd been meaning to chop that tree down for ages – and now the wind has done it for me."

"It wasn't the wind," said Jeremy. "It was Mr Grumff." He was eating his boiled egg.

"Don't speak with your mouth full, Jeremy," replied his father. "Now I must hurry. It might rain later today." He hurried outside.

Jeremy heard the tractor spluttering out of the farm-yard. He knew why it was going so fast. The corn had to be cut and put in the barns quickly, because rain would spoil it.

He finished his egg, and turned the empty shell upside down in the egg cup to make it look like a fresh one. Then he put on his strongest shoes and his oldest jumper. He ran out of the farmyard, then past the two empty barns that were waiting for the corn.

There was the fat oak-tree lying on the ground. Its twisted roots stuck up into the air, well clear of the path. They couldn't trip people any more.

Jeremy began to walk by. Then he saw something hanging from a broken branch. It was something he recognised.

He looked at it and thought. Then he ran back to the farm-house for something. Soon he was hurrying through the corn-fields. He was too busy to help his father just yet.

He ran across the wooden bridge. The water was quiet and slow; in winter it was fast and loud, he remembered. He only glanced at the rabbit-holes in the first glade. He didn't stop at the mushrooms in the second. He went straight to the third.

The giant was awake today. He was sitting on the grass on the far side. Jeremy walked across.

"Hello, Mr Grumff," he said. "Thank you for pulling up the oak-tree. Now it can't give me any more bumps."

"Grumff," mumbled the giant.

"I can't stop long today," went on Jeremy. "I've got to help my father with the corn, before the rain spoils it all."

"Grumff," said the giant gloomily.

"What's the matter, Mr Grumff?" asked Jeremy. "Does your finger still hurt?"

The giant shook his head. He pointed to his boot. It was loose and floppy on his foot; his bootlace had caught on something and had broken in two.

"You did that on the oak-tree," said Jeremy. "I saw a bit of your lace caught on a branch. Look, I've brought you a new one." From under his jumper he pulled out an old clothes-line.

"Grumff-grumff!" said the giant. He began to look much happier.

He took off his floppy boot and pulled out the remains of the broken lace. Then he took one end of the clothes-line and tried to thread it through the lace-holes.

Jeremy watched him. "You can keep the clothes-line, Mr Grumff," he said. "We've got a new one at home."

The giant said nothing. He tried again to push the end of the clothes-line into the lace-hole. He missed. Again he tried, and again he missed. His eyes began to water. A tear landed at Jeremy's feet and splashed his trousers.

The giant muttered something. He pinched the end of the clothes-line hard between his enormous fingers, changed it to his other hand and tried it that way. Again he missed. And again. And again.

"Grumff!" he bellowed angrily. He threw the clothes-line and boot down on to the grass. His fingers were too clumsy.

Jeremy could hear something a long way off. It was the tractor in the corn-fields. He stood up.

"I'll have to leave you now, Mr Grumff," he said. "I must help Dad before it rains and spoils the corn."

He picked up the clothes-line and carefully threaded it through all the lace-holes in the giant's boot. "There, Mr Grumff," he declared. "That's as good as new now."

The giant stared. He picked up his boot and peered at it closely. Then he smiled. Then he chuckled. "Grumff-grumff!"

he said delightedly. He pulled his boot on and tied the lace. His face beaming, he began to march up and down the glade, stamping happily. The trees quivered and the ground shook.

"Giants are very strong," said Jeremy to himself. "They're so strong, they can do anything. Except pull out thorns and thread boot-laces, of course."

Then he walked back through the woods to help his father.

\*        \*        \*

Jeremy spent the afternoon riding on the tractor, watching the harvester clattering along behind. Round and round each corn-field they went, leaving rows of corn-sheaves lying behind them.

But the faster his father drove, the darker the clouds became. And by the time the last field was cut, the sky was black and spots of rain were starting to land on Jeremy's head.

His father drove the tractor back to the farm. As they passed each field, he glanced anxiously at the hundreds of sheaves spread on the ground. "We must get them into the barns at once," he said.

But the moment they reached the farm, the rain began to pour. It came down in torrents and Jeremy and his father had to run into the house.

Sadly they stood at the window and watched. The clouds became thicker and blacker. The rain fell faster and faster. It ran down the window-pane in streams, until it was difficult to see out properly.

"Just look at that cloud over there," said Jeremy's father suddenly. "I can't see it clearly, but it seems as tall as a giant – and it's sweeping across every one of my fields. It's going to soak every sheaf of corn there is."

Jeremy peered hard through the window. Then he smiled. That clothes-line had been a good idea; Mr Grumff was striding as firmly as ever. . . .

*　　　*　　　*

It rained hard all through the night. It did not stop until breakfast, which Jeremy's father ate quietly and sadly. Then he hurried out to see his fields.

He was back in less than a minute. "The two barns are full of sheaves!" he gasped. "Someone brought them in last night; they're hardly wet at all."

Jeremy put on his Wellington boots and followed him out into the farm-yard. They trod through thick mud. They splashed through deep puddles. They stopped before the two barns.

Inside were hundreds of corn-sheaves. They were heaped all in a tangle, as if someone had swept them up with a gigantic broom.

"It must have been another strong wind, I suppose," muttered Jeremy's father, scratching his head in bewilderment.

"No," said Jeremy. "It was just Mr Grumff."

His father was not listening. "Just look over there!" he said suddenly.

He was pointing at the steep hill beyond the fields. Jeremy saw that it was brown instead of green. At the foot of it was a huge pile of earth and rocks.

"A landslide!" declared his father. "All that rain has made the hillside come loose, and the soil and rocks have slithered down. What a storm it must have been! I wonder if any of my sheds became damaged…" And he strode off to find out.

Jeremy began to splash his way through the fields. They were very soggy. His Wellingtons kept sinking in and making a lovely squelchy sound when he pulled them out.

He crossed the bridge over the river. Then he stopped, because something was wrong. Something was missing.

"What is it?" he thought.

Then he remembered. The river should be full of last night's rain, roaring and racing as it had done last winter. But now it was only whispering.

He peered over the side of the bridge. Why, there was even less water than yesterday! Where had the rest gone?

He looked up the valley, to where the river came from. And there in the distance he saw the pile of rocks that had slid down the hillside. The landslide had fallen into the water. The river was nearly blocked.

Jeremy knew what that meant. Instead of pouring along the valley, the river would have to turn sideways and rush down the first slope it could find. Soon it would be flooding across the fields, hurrying towards the farm-house.

Jeremy thought hard. He could run back and tell his father; then his father could use the tractor to move the landslide and let the river go its usual way. But that would take a very long time, and some of the rocks looked too heavy for even a tractor to move. In fact, Jeremy could think of only one thing strong enough to lift them.

He ran into the thick wood. He rushed past the rabbit-holes

in the first glade, and heard somebody say "Ow!" a long way off. He rushed past the mushrooms in the second glade, and heard somebody say "Ow!" a little nearer. He rushed into the third glade and heard somebody say "Ow!" very close indeed.

It was the giant. He was sitting on the grass. He had one arm round the back of his neck, holding a pair of garden shears.

*Snip* they went. "Ow!" cried the giant, clutching his ear.

Jeremy realised what was happening. The giant was trying to cut the hair round his neck, where it was long and tangled and uneven. But it was very difficult, especially without a mirror to help; so it was not surprising that he kept snipping his ear as well.

*Snip* went the shears. And "Ow!" cried the giant again, holding his ear. It did look sore.

"Mr Grumff," cried Jeremy. "A landslide has blocked the river and it's going to flood our farm at any minute. Can you please come and stop it? And I'll cut your hair for you afterwards, if you like, without snipping you one little bit."

"Grumff-grumff!" said the giant. He began to look much happier.

He slipped the shears into his pocket and rose to his feet, making the sky dark. Then he strode off over the trees.

Jeremy felt the ground shake with every step. One . . . Two . . . Three . . . Four . . . The shaking stopped.

Jeremy listened hard. Then he heard a rumbling and a thudding and a swooshing. It sounded as if huge rocks were being tossed aside, and tons of earth being pushed away; and then came the sound of running water, the river gurgling happy and free once more. . . .

The ground started to tremble again. One . . . Two . . . Three . . . Four . . . The giant came striding over the trees, darkening

the sky a second time. He was dusting his hands and lumps of earth landed round Jeremy like hailstones.

"Grumff," declared the giant. He pushed the shears into Jeremy's arms.

"Thank you very much, Mr Grumff," said Jeremy. "My father will be glad when I tell him. Now you must lie on your tummy on the grass and I'll climb on your neck."

And although it was the very first time Jeremy had given anyone a hair-cut with garden shears, he didn't snip the giant's ears even once. And when he said "Good-bye" afterwards, and the giant had said "Grumff-grumff," very gratefully, Jeremy took the shears with him to get them sharpened at home ready for next time.

When Jeremy reached the bridge, he found the river roaring and racing underneath just as it had done last winter. He looked up the valley and saw that the rocks had been tossed aside, as if they had been only a handful of pebbles.

"And that proves it," said Jeremy to himself as he walked on through the fields. "It proves that a giant can do anything."

He reached the farmyard gate and thought for a minute. Then he said: "Well – anything except hair-cutting – and threading boot-laces – and getting thorns out of fingers."

Then he went home.